Minikid

Michael Morpurgo

Minikid

With illustrations by

Faye Hanson

Barrington Stoke

Published in 2014 in Great Britain by
Barrington Stoke Ltd
18 Walker Street, Edinburgh, EH3 7LP

www.barringtonstoke.co.uk

Text © 1974 Michael Morpurgo
Illustrations © Faye Hanson

A CIP catalogue record for this book is available
from the British Library upon request

ISBN: 978-1-78112-352-2

Printed in China by Leo

This book has dyslexia friendly features

Contents

Chapter 1
Menace

The summer I was ten, our cousin Billy came to stay with us. I heard Mum and Dad talking about how his mum and dad were having problems. Mum said Billy would have to live with us for a while until they sorted things out. Dad said that could take for ever and a day.

Me and Lisa were meant to help look after Billy, but I wasn't sure about him.

He was a menace, there was no doubt about that. Bullet, they called him at school. We called him Minikid, and mini he was. He stood about three foot tall in his shoes. He had a head shaped like a cannonball and a body built like a tank.

Chapter 2
A Cloud of Wasps

Until we found the nest, it was one of those good days.

It was a Sunday in August. Dad was flat out in his deckchair with his newspaper over his face and "Sounds of the 70s" blaring out of the radio next to him.

The four of us were mucking about with a hose at the bottom of the garden – me, my sister Lisa, my mate Tom and Minikid.

Lisa was on the attack, which was no problem because she always shut her eyes when she aimed.

She sprayed a tree stump beside
the vegetable patch. And then, all of
a sudden, she dropped the hose and
screamed. Wasps poured out of the

stump – a cloud of them. They sounded
angry and we didn't wait to find out
if they were. We ran for the house,
screaming and laughing all the way.

In the safety of the kitchen, we looked out. The wasps were gone.

"Let's burn them out," I said.

"Yeah, let's burn them," Minikid said. His eyes lit up like a daredevil's.

"No," Lisa said. "You mustn't. Dad gets Mr Holton to do it. It's dangerous."

"She's right, Chris, you know," Tom said. "Mr Holton keeps bees. He knows how to do it." There was a know-all tone in his voice, and I didn't like the way they had ganged up on me. They'd been doing that a lot the last while.

"Just because you're scared," I said.

Tom looked at me – he was angry now.

"Scared?" he said. His top lip quivered.

"Don't be silly, Chris," Lisa joined in.

"Yes. Scared. That's what I said. Scared." I was shouting now.

"Right," said Tom, and he rushed past me. Lisa followed him. Minikid was running next to Tom. He wanted to be part of whatever happened next.

Chapter 3
On the Attack

My face was all hot and I felt angry with myself for being angry. I saw them walk down the garden. Lisa was hurrying after Tom and Minikid, and Minikid was trying to get Tom to let him carry the fuel can too. Lisa was running to keep up and she kept tugging at Tom's shirt.

They walked up to the tree stump slowly and Tom turned to Lisa and pushed her away. He undid the top of the fuel can and walked on his tip-toes to two or three feet away from the stump.

Minikid grabbed the can out of Tom's hands and rushed across to the tree with it. Then he threw it ... once ... twice ...

There was a pause and then I saw
Minikid drop the can. His hands went
up to his face and he started to run and
scream at the same time. There were

swarms of wasps all around him. He
was hitting at them and screaming,
screaming. He reached the back door
with Lisa and Tom close behind him.

"The tap! The tap!" Tom yelled as he came in.

Minikid's hands were grabbing at his face. He was barging about, even more like an angry bull than ever. I turned on the cold tap and pushed his head under. Tom and I kept hitting at his head, to try to kill the wasps for him.

Dad ran in, with his newspaper still in his hand.

"What the devil's going on?" he stormed, and then he saw Minikid bending over the sink.

"It was the wasps, Dad," Lisa blurted out. "They attacked him, hundreds of them. They wouldn't stop."

Dad led Minikid to the sofa in the sitting room. I could see Minikid's face now – it was pale white with big red marks on his cheeks and forehead. Dad took off Minikid's T-shirt and shook it.

There must have been a dozen dead wasps in there and Dad picked more out of his hair. Minikid lay there, quiet and trembling. I didn't dare look at him, and Lisa and Tom weren't looking at me.

"Hospital, I think," Dad said. "I'd better take him to the hospital in town."

Chapter 4
A Trip to Hospital

Minikid sat in the back of the car with Tom and Lisa on the way to the hospital. I sat in front with Dad.

"How did it happen, then?" Dad said.

"We were playing with the hose and we sprayed the nest by mistake," Tom said. "So I thought I'd burn them out. It was my fault." His voice was quiet. Minikid said nothing.

I couldn't look round. I wanted to, but I couldn't.

"That was a crazy thing to do," Dad said. "You should have told me and I could have called Mr Holton. He always does the wasp nests and the bee swarms. You knew that, didn't you, Chris?"

After that, Dad wouldn't let us help out with jobs on the farm. He said we got under his feet, and that we couldn't be trusted any more. He was right. We couldn't be trusted. Especially not with Minikid being such a menace.

Chapter 5
Harvest Time

When it came to harvest time and Minikid hadn't gone home yet, things were different. Dad said that he needed all hands on deck and that we were to help.

We loaded straw bales on to the carts in the hot sun and sat up against the dusty tractor wheel and drank bottles of orange juice. As the evening came on, we murdered mozzies and gnats in their thousands.

After one day like this, we were walking home with Dad when we heard a cow bellow in the shed by the Dutch barn.

"That's Dolly on her fourth calf," Dad said. "She had a hard time of it last year." He hit at the flies.

By the time we reached the shed, Lisa, Minikid and me, Dolly had stopped her bellowing. She was lying down by the far wall. She was huge.

"What a weight to carry around. Looks as if the bottom will fall out of her any minute," I said.

"She must be so uncomfortable," said Lisa.

Minikid stood there and gawped. His mouth hung open to catch the flies. I don't think he'd seen a cow in such a state before.

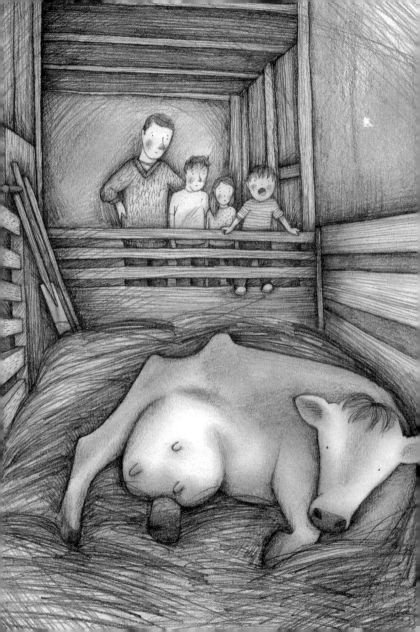

"It'll all be over by the morning.
Dolly will feel better then," I told him.

Dolly went on bellowing all night, an
urgent cry you couldn't ignore.

Chapter 6
Dolly and Her Calf

We were in the middle of breakfast when Dad came in from the milking.

"We lost Dolly," he said, as he washed his hands. "She couldn't take it, poor old thing. But she had a pretty little bull-calf."

"What'll happen to the calf, Dad?"
Lisa said. She had stopped eating.

"Not much chance, love," Dad said.
"He's very weak. We shouldn't have lost
old Dolly. Good milker she was. That's
life, I suppose." Dad sat down and tucked
into his cornflakes.

Lisa's chair screeched as she jumped up. "Where is he, Dad?"

"What, the calf? He's in with Rosie beyond the milking sheds. Why? What ...?"

But Lisa was out of the door, and Dad was left spluttering with a mouthful of soggy cornflakes.

Minikid and I grabbed our toast and ran out after Lisa. When we reached the shed, she was on her knees in the mucky straw, stroking a tiny calf. I climbed over and Minikid lumbered after me.

"Wow," Minikid said. "A real baby cow. Can we play with him?"

Lisa and I ignored him. Dad was right – the calf was pretty. He had a little black turned-up nose and great brown eyes surrounded by long black eyelashes. His coat was soft and beautifully coloured – light brown and fawn.

"Isn't he beautiful?" Lisa said. It was clear she didn't need an answer. "Rosie just ignores him. Look." Sure enough, Rosie was suckling her own calf born two days before, and not taking any heed of the orphan calf.

"He'll die," Lisa said. "Unless we do something."

"Will he?" Minikid said. He looked shocked and excited at the same time.

"We could bottle-feed him," I said. "It might work, but he looks very weak."

We rushed back to ask Dad, who was still eating his breakfast.

"Chris," he said. "I wouldn't bother. I don't think it'll work."

"Oh, please, Dad," Lisa said. "We must try. We can't just let him die, can we?"

Chapter 7
Bottle Feeding

In the end, Dad let us look after the calf.

He told us all what we'd need to do for the feeding – three feeds a day of powdered milk. Wash out the bottle in boiling water after each feed.

We moved the calf back to the shed he'd been born in and put down clean straw. We warmed his first feed and Lisa tried to dribble the milk into the side of his mouth.

Minikid and I watched as for ten minutes he just let it dribble out on to the straw. Nothing had gone in.

"Let me have a go," I said. I sat down, held his head and pushed the bottle into his mouth.

His great eyes looked at me without blinking. Then, all of a sudden, a long, grey tongue crept out to lick his nose, which was covered in milk. He licked and almost right away he started to suck.

"He's doing it!" Lisa said. "He's doing it!"

"I want a go! I want a go!" Minikid shouted. He did a wild dance in the straw.

We let him take over and the calf finished off that bottle.

A lot was lost, but never mind.

He took the other two feeds that day, and for the last one he stood up on very wobbly legs. His little black birth-cord was still dangling from his middle.

When we put him to bed that night, we knew he'd be all right.

Chapter 8
Bambi

Jersey calves often look like deer when they're young, and our one definitely did.

We called him Bambi, and he went from strength to strength.

After four days of bottle feeding, he started on a bucket and took to it with no trouble.

Now, when we went to see him, we found him skipping around his shed like a baby lamb. Two dark rings of black grew around his eyes – he looked as if he was wearing glasses.

He sucked your hand until it was sore, and when you pulled it out, it dripped with saliva. Then he'd try your trouser leg, or your sleeve or your foot, anything he could get hold of.

He'd pretend to be a Spanish fighting bull and butt you with his soft, hornless head. Minikid loved that and would try to butt him back. They were two baby bulls together.

We spent the last three weeks of our holidays looking after Bambi. It was odd, but Dad didn't seem interested in him and even Mum always seemed to change the subject if Bambi ever came up in conversation.

Chapter 9
The Holidays Are Over

And then it was our first day back at school. We had to take Minikid with us and he was as much of a menace as ever.

Jimmy Tyler grabbed him and tried his favourite trick of shutting him in the playground toilets.

Minikid came storming out, flailing his arms and screaming in anger. He was a proper hero. But he was still a menace.

We couldn't wait for the day to be over so we could get back and see Bambi. We ran all the way home and, as usual, Lisa got there first.

6

"He's not there, Chris," she cried. "The shed is empty. They must have put him with the others."

We searched through all the sheds and pens. Minikid was on the rampage, as usual. Nothing. No Bambi.

We ran up to the house and found Mum back from work.

"Mum," Lisa said. "What's happened to Bambi? He's not in his shed. Someone's moved him and we can't find him anywhere."

Lisa was trying to stop herself crying – I could see that.

"Lisa, now calm down," Mum said, and she took her by the arms. "He's gone to market, love, this morning. Your father did try to warn you. He's a bull-calf, a Jersey bull-calf. He's no use to us here, you see."

"But, Mum, what'll happen to him?"
I said.

"I know, I know," yelled Minikid.
"They kill them, they kill them dead."

"Shut up!" cried Lisa. "They
slaughter them, don't they, Mum? Don't
they?" She was shouting now. I'd never
seen her so angry.

"They don't feel anything, Lisa. It's quite humane," Mum said, and she turned away.

But Minikid wouldn't shut up. "I bet it hurts," he kept saying. "I bet Bambi won't like it one bit."

When Dad came in that evening, we went to bed. Neither of us spoke to him for over a week.

We didn't much feel like playing with Minikid either, after that.

Chapter 10
Goodbye, Minikid

The next week, we were all pleased when Minikid's mum and dad came and took him home. We didn't miss him too much, not after what had happened with Bambi.

Also by
Michael Morpurgo ...

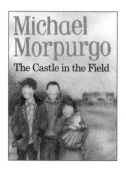

**It wasn't really a castle. It was a pill-box – an
old army guard post from World War Two.
And it was the best hide-out ever.**

Chris, Lisa and Tom love the Castle. But the Castle
is on Old Rafferty's land. Old Rafferty dislikes
everyone, and children even more. How long can
Chris, Lisa and Tom keep their hide-out a secret?

**Snug was Lisa's cat.
No one ever gave him to her.
They just grew up together.**

Snug came home with Lisa's dad when Lisa was
a baby. Soon Lisa and Snug were the best of
friends. But Snug's a tom cat, and tom cats like their
freedom ...

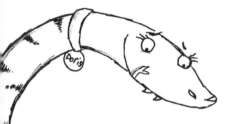

Have you read the other Little Gems?

The Moonshine Dragon
Little Gems
Cornelia Funke

Sea Urchins and Sand Pigs
Little Gems
Cornelia Funke

Blamehounds
Little Gems
Ross Collins

MARY'S HAIR
Little Gems
EOIN COLFER

Malorie Blackman
My Friend's a Gris-Kwok

THE First Third WISH
Ian Beck

GO! GO! CHI CHICO!
Little Gems
Geraldine McCaughrean

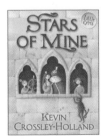

Cheesemares
Little Gems
Ross Collins

STARS OF MINE
Little Gems
KEVIN CROSSLEY-HOLLAND